A Bride for Braxton

Oakdale Romance Duet

Book 1

CHERYL WRIGHT

Contents:

A BRIDE FOR BRAXTON

OAKDALE ROMANCE DUET

BOOK 1

Copyright 2018 by Cheryl Wright

Previously published as May in Calendar Men
Series

Thanks

Thanks to my very dear friends (and authors), Margaret Tanner and Susan Horsnell.

Without their encouragement and help, I would never have embarked on this amazing journey.

Thanks also to Alan, my husband of over 44 years, who has been a relentless supporter of my writing for many years.

About the Author

Multi-published, best selling and award-winning author, Cheryl Wright, former secretary, debt collector, account manager, writing coach, and shopping tour hostess, loves reading.

She writes both contemporary and historical western romance, as well as contemporary romance and romantic suspense.

She lives in Melbourne, Australia, and is married with two adult children and has six grandchildren.

When she's not writing, she can be found in her craft room making greeting cards.

Check out Cheryl's Amazon page - https://www.amazon.com/author/cherylwright for a full list of her other books.

Other Links:

http://cheryl-wright.com

https://www.facebook.com/cherylwrightauthor

Newsletter

http://cheryl-wright.com/newsletter.html

Chapter One

"Y ou did what?" Braxton Chalmers could feel the heat travel up his face.

If he thought his cousin Melanie was pushy before, he now saw her with a whole new perspective.

He sat opposite her, his hands on his knees as he leaned forward, waiting impatiently for her explanation.

All the while his foot tapped nervously.

"Honestly Brax," she said. "It's not *that* big a deal."

Yeah right. She'd volunteered his time for the local Youth Center's annual fundraiser. He wouldn't have to do much, she said. He'd be standing around a lot, she'd added.

His eyes squinted suspiciously.

She was up to something, but Braxton had absolutely no idea that it was.

Melanie was always up to something and every single time she dragged him into it. He should just break ties with her. But how could he?

They'd grown up together. He loved her as cousins loved each other.

She'd introduced him to his first girlfriend, although it didn't last long, and she'd dated his best mate.

That too hadn't lasted.

She was always concocting something, and he knew, was absolutely convinced, she was up to her neck in it right now.

"It's one night, Brax," she said impatiently. "What's the issue? I know you volunteer there all the time."

"The issue," he said, trying to control his temper. "Is that you didn't ask – you just went ahead and put my name down."

She had the audacity to grin.

Without warning, she jumped out of her chair and headed to the refrigerator where she pulled out a beer and passed it to him.

As if that would pacify him. He was near boiling point and Mel wants to fix things with a beer?

He silently counted to ten, wondering if fifty would be better.

This was nothing new. His dear cousin pulled these types of stunts all the time.

There was the time he thought he was attending a family dinner, but it turned out to be a blind date organized by Mel.

Another time she organized the blind date then told him. The 'date' spent the entire night on her cell.

And then there was the time she..... Nuh, not going there.

He braced his shoulders and glared at her. "What *exactly* am I doing at this fundraiser?"

He didn't trust her one little bit. She'd come up with so many crazy schemes over the years, and right now his *scheme radar* was off the charts.

She shifted in her seat uncomfortably.

He watched closely as the color drained from her face.

Mel shuffled about for nearly a minute, licked her lips, then spoke quietly. "You know, the usual stuff – take tickets at the door, help move tables, that sort of thing."

He sat back in his seat and relaxed. He felt more comfortable now.

And suddenly everything changed.

He studied her as she tried to force back a grin. Her hand suddenly went up to her mouth and she pretended to cough.

Something was definitely up.

He frowned and stared at her. If he did it long enough, she might renege and tell him the whole story?

Without warning she stood. "Sorry cuz," she said quickly, glancing at her watch.

Was she going to own up to her lies after all? He hoped so.

"I've got an appointment in ten. Gotta run."

And that was that. She snatched the near empty beer bottle from his hand and shoved him toward the door, snatching up his cowboy hat as she did so.

"Mel..."

"Sorry, no time. Talk soon." She slammed his hat into his hands, then gave him an almighty shove and banged the door behind him.

He swallowed hard. *What the hell was she up to?*

* * *

"Hey Brax." It was Mel. What did she want now? "I just realized I didn't give you the date of the fundraiser."

He heard her swallow – hard. "May 20. 8:30pm. But I'll need you there an hour early." She said it quickly as though she needed to get it out in a hurry.

"Uh huh." If he kept her talking, he might finally get the truth.

She suddenly changed track. "By the way, Sierra West is in town."

That stopped him in his tracks. He'd dated Sierra when they were teenagers. She was seventeen and he was almost twenty. It felt like a life-time ago.

He recalled how they were practically inseparable; spent almost every waking moment together. He'd even thought about asking her to marry him, despite their young ages.

Then suddenly she left town – for a job in the city. She'd given him no warning whatsoever, and he was shocked when she'd told him the night before she was to leave.

He recalled his agonizing pain at losing her. He'd walked around in a fog for weeks, not understanding what had happened.

He was inconsolable and his heart felt as though it has been shattered into tiny pieces.

Despite all that, he would never forget holding her in his arms, and how it made him feel.

Even after all this time, his traitorous mind still brought those memories to the forefront.

"Her grandmother died," Mel said, bringing him out of his thoughts. "She's back for the funeral."

"Oh." He loved Evelyn dearly, and recalled some of their time spent together. She was such a nice old bird. He'd spent quite a bit of time at her place. He had visited there often while he dated Sierra, even having a number of meals there. "I'm sorry," he said genuinely. "I really liked her."

"You'll get the chance to tell her yourself," Mel said. "I've invited her to dinner. Of course, you'll be coming too."

He reveled in the opportunity to see Sierra again but was annoyed at his cousin for again manipulating him.

"Six o'clock sharp," she said.

Before he could protest, she disconnected the call.

Typical Mel.

As much as he was annoyed with Mel, it would be good to see Sierra again. She would have moved on by now, probably had a husband and 2.5 kids this far down the track.

He did the mental arithmetic. It was a little over ten years since they'd seen each other. She'd visited before, of course, but he'd gone out of his way not to see her.

She was out of reach, and he wasn't going to leave himself open to having his heart crushed again.

He'd thought of following her to the city, of course, but he loved this little town. There was no way he could have left at that time. Nor did he want to leave.

He still didn't.

His heart was here and always would be. Apart from the fact he now had his own business here.

He leaned back in his chair. and wondered what she looked like now, ten years on. Would she have changed much? He thought she probably would have, especially living in the big city, with all the pollution that could be found there.

Had he changed at all?

He strolled over to the hallway mirror and stared at his reflection. He didn't think he'd changed much at all.

Braxton pulled out his cell phone and pulled up a photograph from ten years ago. *The photograph.* The much-loved selfie showed the two of them staring into each other's eyes. Two young people very much in love.

He looked back at his reflection; he hadn't changed much.

A bit older than he was in the photo, his black hair seemed even blacker, if that was possible. The biggest change was probably his stubble.

It was so dark, it was hard to conceal, even after freshly shaving.

He ran his hand across his chin, the way Sierra used to like doing.

He shook himself.

Back in his comfortable lounge chair, he stared at the photograph for a long time. He had regretted their parting from the moment she'd left.

Why hadn't he stopped her? Or at least *tried* to stop her? He hadn't made any attempt to keep her there, and that had played on his mind for some years. Even to this day he regretted not trying to convince her to stay.

But that was all in the past. Things had changed. He'd moved on and assumed Sierra had too.

A quiet knock at the door interrupted his thoughts.

"Brax. Braxton." A familiar voice called out to him at the same time she was knocking.

He braced himself; he'd know that voice anywhere. Sierra stood outside his front door.

He took a deep breath and slowly let it out, then walked toward the door. He put his hand to the door handle but didn't open it for the longest time.

He wasn't sure what his reaction was going to be like, seeing her after such a long passage of time.

By the time he opened the door, she was already walking away. Her back was to him, so she didn't see him standing there.

"Sierra," he called quietly.

She turned toward him, and he watched as her lips quivered, then her eyes filled with tears. He was certain the tears weren't because of him, but for the loss of her dear grandmother, Evelyn.

He opened his arms, as he'd done so many times all those years ago, and she ran to him. He wrapped his arms around her, and they stood there for what seemed forever.

Her tears flowed, and she sobbed her heart out. Through all of that, it felt as though they'd never been apart.

Memories came flooding back as he held her, good memories, from better days. Thoughts of holding her, kissing her, and simply being together.

He held her tight, stroking her silky soft hair as she cried, gently rubbing her back to chase the demons away.

His heart rate accelerated – he'd never forgotten the feel of her in his arms. His heart that had been shattered into a million pieces when she'd left, suddenly felt whole again.

Braxton knew, without a doubt, he had to protect himself, protect his heart. Because once the funeral was over, Sierra would leave him again, as she had done all those years before.

* * *

"I'm sorry," Sierra said, once she'd composed herself again.

He led her to one of the big comfortable chairs in his lounge room. "Don't apologize. It's hard losing someone you love."

She glanced around the room, trying to distract herself. It was obvious to Braxton she felt embarrassed about her outburst.

She stared in the direction of his hat stand. "You've still got that old hat?" She laughed, and he recalled how much he'd loved to hear that tinkling sound when they'd dated.

Braxton studied her. She was still as pretty as she was all those years ago. Little had changed, and to his disgust, he felt as much for her now as he did back then.

He ignored her question. "How long are you here for?"

"I'm staying for the funeral, of course," she said quietly. "But I got extended leave. I've been feeling a bit burned out."

She glanced down into her lap and stared at her entwined hands.

It was then he realized he didn't really know what she did for a living. In fact, he wasn't sure she still worked until now. It would make sense, if she had kids, that she might be a stay at home mom.

He shifted in his seat at the thought of her being a mom.

She looked up and stared at him. "Something wrong?"

He shook his head. "I... I thought you might not work." He took a deep breath, almost anticipating what she would say next.

Instead she frowned. "Why would I not work? I mean, that doesn't even make sense."

He shifted again. "To look after your kids?"

He watched as her expression went from confused to amusement. "Kids? I don't have kids." She leaned forward and stared into his face. "I don't even have a husband," she said quietly.

"You don't? I thought by now…"

"Too busy working," she said. "More's the pity."

Once again, he wished he'd followed her to the big city. Perhaps he might have convinced her to come back home to Oakdale.

But he knew that wasn't true. He wouldn't have done that. Not ever. She had to make her own decisions, and he wouldn't have wanted to have her life choices, or lack thereof, on his conscious.

"I…" She licked her lips, and he remembered the way she used to do that when he was about to kiss her, the way she pouted her lips in readiness.

Her lips were still as enticing and as luscious as they always were. Only now they were painted a pretty soft pink.

"I'm still available," she said quickly and suddenly.

He sat forward. "Really?" He was incredulous. He was convinced this beautiful young woman he once courted would have been snatched up by now.

His heart beat loudly. So loud he could hear it racing in his head. She'd said he had a chance. He opened his mouth to speak, then suddenly came to his senses.

He shook that ridiculous thought out of his head and frowned at her.

"What about you?" she said out of the blue.

His head hurt. Braxton hadn't contemplated this scenario, but now it had presented himself, it gave him pause.

He leaned back in his chair and thought.

Thought about the good times. The places they'd visited together. The quiet times they'd spent just hanging out. The days they'd gone riding up to the hills, just the two of them.

The bad times suddenly reared their ugly head. The way he felt when she said she was leaving. Giving him no warning whatsoever. She was leaving the next day on the train, and she didn't want him to see her off.

He was heartbroken. In many ways he still was. He'd thought about her often for some years, then decided he needed to block her out of his memories. Forever.

"What are you saying," he asked softly.

She waved her hands about in front of her face, then shook her head. "Forget it," she said. "I had this weird idea that things could be how they used to be when we were kids."

He grimaced. He couldn't help it. "I'm single," he suddenly blurted out, then immediately regretted it.

Building a relationship on something that happened over ten years ago couldn't possibly work. Besides, she all but admitted she was only here for the funeral and then some extended leave.

After that she would be gone again. Totally out of his life.

Just like before.

Chapter Two

Sierra arrived early for dinner as planned.

Mel said she wanted to have a 'private chat' before Braxton arrived.

That piqued her interest more than a little.

Melanie glanced over the top of her coffee mug and studied her best friend from their teenage years.

"You're going to help, right?" she said. "Tell me you're going to help." She'd already had four people pull out, which left her short-handed.

It wasn't that Melanie was hard to get along with, it was just that people hadn't realized how much organization was involved in a charity event such as this.

Sierra sighed. "I guess."

Melanie stared at her. "You don't sound very convincing. *Please*," she begged. "You've got to help. I can't do this alone."

Her friend stared at her. "You won't be alone. Mrs Jones is helping, Mrs Squires, and, ah..."

She counted off on her fingers. "Oh, that's right, Mary Jessop offered as well?"

Melanie nodded. "That's right, but that makes just four of us. I really, *really* need your help. Besides, Brax is part of the auction."

Mel grinned at her friend, but Sierra was confused.

She swallowed down a big mouthful of coffee, then almost choked on it. "What do you mean *Brax is part of the auction*? Apart from helping with tables and other stuff, that doesn't even make sense."

"Shhhhh, it's a secret," Mel said, putting her fingers to her lips. "I haven't told him."

Sierra was still confused. "Haven't told him what? I have no idea what you're talking about Melanie."

"If he wasn't my cousin, I'd find Brax pretty darned sexy. And I know you do."

Sierra felt the heat creep up her face. "I can't help it if I find him attractive. He's a good-looking man."

Mel leaned forward excitedly. "Exactly! And that's why I signed him up for the Bachelor Auction."

Sierra's hands suddenly flew to her face. "Oh my." She stared at the other woman. "Does he know?"

Mel suddenly stood. "No, and you're not going to tell him."

"I don't know…."

"Come on, Sierra, I need your help. Please? *Pretty please?*"

She stared at Mel for several moments before answering. "Sure. Why not? Especially since it's for a good cause." She took another sip of her coffee. "I am *not* doing this because Brax will be there."

"Yeah sure," Melanie said, grinning broadly. "Nothing to do with Brax being there."

They both knew Sierra's *crush* had not dissipated one iota.

* * *

The knock at the door had interrupted something, Braxton was certain of it.

Their laughter and chatter drifted through the door and into his ears. He couldn't understand the words, but he could sure as heck hear their voices.

He'd told Mel more than once she needed a stronger door. One that couldn't be easily destroyed in a robbery or attack.

All that had done was frighten her, so he hadn't broached it again. But he was hell-bent on replacing that door for her after tonight.

The voices suddenly stopped, and he heard footsteps approaching moments before the door opened to him.

"Brax." Mel stepped forward and kissed his cheek.

That got his shackles up. She *never* kissed him. Ever. Was she trying to soften him up for whatever it was she was planning?

He shook himself mentally. Surely not?

As he stepped into the hallway, he spotted Sierra. She stood up and walked toward him. They embraced, and she whispered in his ear. "Sorry about earlier."

He brushed her words aside. "It's fine," he whispered back. "You were upset. I can understand that."

She gave him a little squeeze, then ended the hug. He felt bereft as she walked away.

He sighed. This couldn't happen. He wouldn't let it happen. Again.

"We were just talking about the Youth Center Fundraiser," Mel said.

"Hmph." He really wasn't interested. He didn't mind helping the youth center, and as she had already pointed out, he volunteered there all the time.

He even ran trail rides to help the kids out. Some of them came from very dysfunctional families, and it could be the only time they got to see a horse in real life.

Mel busied herself with the last-minute arrangements for dinner, and left Sierra and Braxton to chat.

"So you're going to the fundraiser?" he asked. "I think it will be quite boring," he said low enough that Mel wouldn't hear.

Sierra's hand went to her mouth, which was curious. She straightened her back before answering. "I think it's a great thing you're doing," she told him. "Even if you do run the risk of being bored."

"Who's bored?" Mel re-entered the room, carrying a tray with garlic and herb bread.

"I'm going to be bored at the fundraiser," Brax offered, taking the tray from her and placing it on the table that was already set.

Mel grinned at Sierra and quickly left the room. *Curiouser and curiouser.*

She returned a few minutes later with a huge bowl of spaghetti bolognaise as well as parmesan cheese.

"Sit down, tuck in," she said.

It was a favorite with Braxton. He adored Mel's spag bol, so she often served it when he was around.

"Yum." He grabbed one of the bowls Mel had set out and began to dish up. She glared at him.

He was so used to it just being him and Mel, he hadn't given Sierra a thought. "Ooops, sorry. Ladies first." He waved his hand toward her and stepped back.

Sierra laughed that sweet tinkling laugh that always drew him in.

At least he had the decency to be embarrassed. He could feel his humiliation creeping up his face.

"For a cowboy, you have appalling manners," Sierra said, almost doubling over with laughter. He found himself joining in.

She was still grinning when she sat down to eat. "I was kidding," she said, ensuring he understood her motives.

"Yeah, sure," he said teasingly.

He'd really missed her. Missed her comebacks, her pretty face, and missed her warmth and her hugs. Most of all, he missed Sierra and the way they'd loved each other all those years ago.

He almost choked on his dinner and grabbed the glass of water sitting in front of him. *Why was he thinking that way? He could not get back together with her – she would be leaving before he knew it.*

Sierra jumped up from her seat and slapped him on the back. "Are you okay," she asked, concerned.

He waved his hand around. "I'll be fine," he said between coughs. She stood beside him until she was convinced. He could feel her warmth and it bothered him.

Bothered him that her nearness caused him so much angst. Bothered him that he was still enamored with her after all this time.

And it sure as heck bothered him that all he wanted to do right now was kiss her.

He mentally slapped himself. He'd long been certain he was over his teenage crush from so long ago.

Obviously, he wasn't. He had to get her out of his head, out of his mind, and out of his thoughts.

Memories were good, but not when they enticed you to want to do things that would be counter-productive. Like kissing the woman who left you so long ago. And fully knowing that woman would be leaving again in a few weeks time.

He glanced sideways at her. She still looked concerned. "I'm alright," he said. "Honestly." He reached across and took a piece of garlic bread, then passed the basket to her.

"I'll take herb, thanks. You never know who I might be kissing later tonight," she said, laughing.

His hand stopped mid-air with the garlic bread in his hand. *Should he partake?*

He felt four eyes trained on him. "Haha, good one," he said, smirking, then took a huge bite out of the offending item.

During dinner they talked a little about the fundraiser, and Mel gave him a bit more insight into what she needed from him.

"Honestly, Brax," she said, studying him. "Move tables around, help with ticket sales. Maybe even help take drink orders and deliver them."

"Uh huh." He was still convinced there was far more to this than meets the eye. Mel being Mel, there had to be.

"We might need you to help with the higher-up decorations too. With your height, that would be a Godsend."

Yeah, being over six foot did sometimes have its advantages.

"So what's the attraction this year," he asked, hoping he'd finally get a *real* answer.

Mel stopped eating long enough to answer. "The auction," she said blandly. "It's always about the auction."

He glanced sideways again, and Sierra's eyes were opened wide. Something was up, only now Sierra was in on the act.

He put his fork into his bowl and placed his hands on the table. Time to get forceful. "Right," he said almost angrily. "Time for the truth. What the *hell* is going on?"

Mel stood. "Nothing dear cousin," she said quietly. "What makes you think that?" She went to the other side of the table and kissed his cheek. Again.

He squinted. It got more and more suspicious by the minute.

As she walked away, he grabbed her hand. "Mel," he said between gritted teeth. "If you're lying to me, so help me..."

She turned back to him. "Me? Lie to you? Never!"

He caught a glimpse of her grin as she faced Sierra. Those two were definitely in cahoots, and he only had a short time to find out what it was.

Come May 20, all would be revealed.

He was developing a headache. Mel had really outdone herself this time, he was certain of it.

Chapter Three

Braxton liked to relax with a coffee before he started work on his horse property *Whispering Pines.*

He loved to sit outside and watch the sunrise – it was one of his favorite pastimes. He had a policy to relax before the busy day ahead. It was the thing that prevented burn-out. At least he believed it did.

After gulping down the last few mouthfuls, he returned his mug to the kitchen, then headed for the stables.

"Morning everyone," he said as he walked through the door.

"Morning, Boss," his Property Manager replied from inside a stall.

Braxton smiled. It was usually just him and the horses at this hour, so he was a bit startled to get a response. "You're early, Austin," he quipped, not giving away his surprise.

The other man stepped into view and shrugged his shoulders. "Couldn't sleep, so thought I might as well come to work."

Braxton reached for the brush before saddling his horse. Once he was done, he added the horse blanket, then saddled his horse, Amos. "Easy boy," he said, as the horse backed away. The beast was a bit skittish this morning.

Reaching into his pocket he pulled out a chunk of apple. Amos greedily snatched it up and allowed his master to finally outfit him.

Pulling the cinch a little tighter, Braxton put the bridle on the now distracted horse, and led him out of the stables with a firm grip on the reins. Amos was not himself today.

Once outside, the reason was clear. Sierra stood at the fence, waiting for them to appear. Amos generally didn't mind people, but he always sensed when something was wrong or different.

And this was not the norm.

He braced himself. The more he saw Sierra, the more comfortable he felt with her. And that was the last thing he wanted.

She stared across at him, the early morning sunlight glistening in her dusty blonde hair, which she'd tied up in a sweet bun.

He slowly looked her over from top to toe. She smiled as she noticed him looking, and he grinned. "Like what you see?" she asked, obviously amused.

Laughing, he walked toward her, Amos trailing behind. "Boots and all. I guess you never forget." His thoughts went back to the first time she'd come to this place. She was sixteen. *Sweet sixteen and never been kissed.* He soon fixed that.

He'd invited her out to see what a real ranch looked like. She was a city kid – had lived in Oakdale all her life.

Not the *real* city mind you, just their quaint little outback town. But that had always been city to him.

His parents had owned the property back then. They'd since retired and let him buy it for a song. He'd worked hard to maintain what had been passed onto him.

His mind went back to the boots: the first time Sierra had visited, she'd worn boots. Bright red stiletto boots. The kind you would wear to a disco or a party. Or perhaps a music festival.

It had tickled his funny bone and he'd stood there laughing at her. She didn't see the joke. Instead she put her hands on her hips, pouted, and said a few choice words.

His mother saved the day by offering *her* boots for Sierra to wear.

Today's boot were much more sensible. Black gumboots.

She trotted over to him and Amos in her two sizes too big boots, her feet swishing this way and that.

He stifled a grin.

"Don't even say it," she said gruffly.

He covered his mouth as the grin threatened to break through. "Me? Say something untoward? Never!"

A tiny smile crept onto her face, and then it became a grin. "I borrowed them from Gran's place. They were my grandad's."

Her smile faded, and her eyes glistened with unshed tears. "I think I need a hug," she said quietly, as she moved closer to her ex.

His heart beat rapidly. *He didn't want to do this.* But really, he did.

Every time he touched her, he felt as though all the years had dropped away.

She leaned into him, her head resting on his shoulder. "I really missed you, Brax," she said softly.

His lips against her hair, his answer came out muffled. "I missed you too. More than words can say." He hoped she hadn't heard him – he hadn't meant to say it out loud.

She bent her head back and looked up at him. "You did?" She sighed and leaned into him once more.

Without thinking he stroked her back. "Sweet Sierra," he said softly.

Her head went back once again. "You haven't called me that for years," she said, staring into his eyes.

"Only because you weren't here to hear it," he said. He stared down into her face. Those beautiful coppery eyes that got him every time.

He pulled his gaze away and surveyed her lips. They were full and luscious, and he couldn't resist any longer. Before he knew what he was doing, his lips covered hers.

There was a buzz in the air, all over his body too. His mouth tingled, and his brain was a fog. His sweet Sierra was home, had come back to him.

"Brax? Is this a good idea?" Her words were muffled, and he could barely make them out.

He stepped back from her. "You're right of course. I'm sorry – it won't happen again, I promise." He wiped a hand across his stubbled chin, then studied her.

"I..." She looked bewildered, disheveled, and he had no doubt why. That kiss should never have happened.

"Did you come out here for something specific," he asked abruptly.

She straightened up, seemed to get control of her thoughts then. "I came to tell you the funeral is tomorrow. 2pm." She brushed a loose strand of hair back behind her ear. Just as well, otherwise he would have done it – the temptation was there, and he was fighting with himself to abstain.

"I know, I'll be there," he said. "I really liked your gran. Besides," he said. "I want to be there for you."

She focused on something behind him and nodded. "I appreciate that," she said, and began to walk away.

"How long since you've ridden," he said quickly, guessing it was ten years ago. Not many places in the city to ride.

She turned to him and the sunlight played off her eyes, reminding him of another time, forever ago. "Last time I was here. A very long time ago," she said softly. "I really missed this place."

He missed her being here too but couldn't dwell on it. She was leaving again soon, too soon for his liking, so they had to pretend they didn't feel anything for each other, and make-believe they were just good friends.

"I'm sure Amos wouldn't mind." He studied her – *was she going to refuse?* She was a city girl now. A real, fair dinkum city girl.

He watched as she wared with herself, until finally, she stepped forward. "Sure, why not," she said, coming to stand before the placid horse. "I'm not sure I remember how to get on." She flashed him a half smile, and he grinned. That was so Sierra.

"Left foot in the left stirrup, hold the reins and the saddle horn, then swing over." He put his hands to her hips to help her up. "Hang onto tight the reins."

She did a funny little skip, and Amos stepped back and whinnied. "Easy boy." He held tighter to her hips as she nearly fell. "Let's try that again, only this time, hold firmly to the reins, and let him know who's boss."

She nodded slightly then placed her foot in the stirrup as instructed. This time she managed to mount the horse. Amos whinnied, stepped backwards again.

Once she was properly seated and seemed settled, he took over the reins and began to walk her around the paddock. "You okay up there?" he tossed over his shoulder.

"Sure am," she said, looking very comfortable, just like she had all those years ago.

Braxton inwardly berated himself. He was falling for Sierra all over again. And that just wouldn't do.

* * *

Feeling uncomfortable in his suit and tie, Braxton slid into a pew at the back of the tiny chapel. He desperately wanted to be inconspicuous, yet still being there for his friend, Sierra.

She'd spotted him the moment she stepped inside, her arm linked with Melanie's. The two were after all, best friends, going back decades.

"Brax?" Sierra had near glared at him. "What are you doing there? I need you down the front with me."

Him? Down the front where the family traditionally sit?

It was as though she'd read his thoughts. "Yes, you silly. You were like family back then. Gran would want you to be there."

His heart thudded. He suddenly felt guilty. He'd visited Evelyn regularly since Sierra had left, but he'd let that lapse the past few months since she'd moved into the nursing home. "No, I can't," he said quietly. "I let her down. I can't sit in the family area." He could barely breathe due to the lump in his throat.

She glared at him. "Dammit, Braxton," she spat out, albeit quietly. "I need you today. *Please* sit with me."

Sierra looked ready to burst into tears. Today was going to be difficult for her, and he was making it even harder.

He stood, and she wrapped her arms around him in a big hug. "Thank you," she whispered.

The three made their way to the front of the chapel and took their seats. He was shaken to the core when he looked across and saw the highly polished coffin sitting to the side, covered in flowers.

He swallowed hard. He might not have seen her in the past three months, but Evelyn would always hold a place in his heart. Braxton reached across and covered Sierra's hand with his own. He squeezed it gently to let her know he was there to support her.

Through her tears, she smiled tentatively.

As the service ended, they stood. She leaned against him for support, and he put his arm around her back, worried she might collapse.

If it hadn't been for Evelyn, he didn't know what would have happened to Sierra. Her parents had died when she was very young, and Evelyn had taken on her upbringing. She was like a mother to Sierra.

As they walked slowly down the aisle, out into the carpark area, tears continued to stream down her face. There was little he could do except be there for her.

He knew as little as it was, it meant a lot to Sierra.

Chapter Four

The funeral had come and gone.

He'd been there for her, and to see her beloved grandmother off. He'd spent a lot of time with Evelyn when he and Sierra were dating. He'd made it a point to visit her at least once a month – all this time, over all those years.

He'd visited her a few times after she'd moved into the nursing home and wished now, he'd visited more often. Life can be gone in a flash, and it can leave you with deep regrets.

He'd told himself it was because between his trail ride business and the horse breeding, there wasn't a lot of time left. But he knew it was because every time he visited her, it reminded him of Sierra. He'd been selfish.

Evelyn's beautiful old house had stood empty from the moment she'd left. Sierra told him, she'd been and aired it out a few times since she'd moved out, but otherwise it stood there totally forlorn.

Such a shame.

He'd offered to take Sierra back to the old mansion because she didn't want to go there alone, but she'd wanted to sort out a few things.

She pulled out her key and unlocked the door. It creaked as it opened.

The musty smell hit him the moment they stepped inside. He wandered purposely over to the windows and threw them open.

"The smell is a bit overwhelming," he said, almost coughing from the dust floating around.

Sierra stood in the middle of the room and gazed around. She closed her eyes and stood there for about two minutes before answering. He wondered what she was thinking.

"It is that. I've really neglected this place. I should have opened it up periodically."

Regret was written all over her face.

He moved toward her and put an arm around her shoulder. "It's not your fault. You've been living in the big city," he said quietly. "Hell, I could have done it for you, but I just didn't think."

She stared into his face. "It wasn't your job, it was mine."

Even so, he could have helped. He'd once loved this woman and her grandmother. Had spent a big chunk of his teenage years right here in this house.

His arm dropped away.

"What happens to the house now?"

"It...." She spotted something, and bent over, reaching into one of the packing boxes sitting in the middle of the room. She pulled out a sunhat. "Gran's hat," she said, holding it tightly against her chest, tears welling in her eyes.

She closed her eyes again. More tightly this time. "Do you remember the first time you came here," she asked.

How could he forget? Evelyn was a forbidding woman. Braxton was even a little afraid of her. She'd told him in no uncertain terms that he'd better not hurt her granddaughter, or there'd be hell to pay.

He smiled.

"What are you thinking about?"

He looked up at her. "The first time I met Evelyn, and she threatened me. Remember?"

"How could I forget. I thought you were going to slink right out that door again." She laughed, and he joined in.

"It didn't seem it at the time, but it's pretty funny when you look back."

Sierra grinned. "You were already well over six foot at that point, and Gran was five-two. And yet you were intimidated."

"She was scary, your gran." He ran his hands over his chin.

"No she wasn't."

He studied her. "You're right. She really wasn't, but the first time I met her, she made sure I was scared." He laughed, then dropped his voice to a quiet whisper. "She really loved you, Sierra. But I think you know that already."

She nodded but didn't speak, continuing to rifle through the packing box. "I'm not sure what to do with the house."

She turned her head away, not meeting his gaze. "She left you the house?" He whistled low and long.

Sierra's voice was only just above a whisper. "What else could she do with it except leave it to a charity or something? I'm the only family she had left."

He really hadn't thought about it. "Are you keeping it, or selling it?"

"I, I'm not sure." She put all the items she'd picked up back into the packing box. "I should have sorted this lot out ages ago. But I was so busy with work."

She looked upwards. "I'm really sorry, Gran," she said, a tear trickling down her face.

Braxton moved to her side and hugged her. "I wish I'd left my job and spent more time with her. Now it's too late," she said, a sob forcing itself to the surface.

He pulled her closer, held her tighter. "I hate that job," she spat. "I've hated it for a very long time."

Mel had told him she worked at a hotel in the big city, but that was about all. "What do you do?" he asked quietly.

She pushed back from him, and he watched as she tried to compose herself. She pulled out a tissue and blew her nose and stared at him.

Despite her red puffy eyes, and her very red nose, she was still beautiful. She always was, and always would be in his eyes.

"Hotel Manager," she said softly. "I left town to take up an internship there and worked my way up the ladder. Only now I hate being there. It took me away from everything I loved – this town, Gran, you…"

She stared at him, and he just stood there, dumbfounded. They were only kids, they'd had their whole lives ahead of them.

Despite that, he'd mourned her loss for years, until he decided he had to move on. Only he hadn't been able to.

He'd dated several women over the years, but they weren't Sierra. No one could ever live up to her memory, and that nearly killed him. So, he'd stopped dating and had thrown himself into his work instead.

He'd been voted *The Most Eligible Bachelor* a few years back in the local rag, which only served to get his back up. He was so angry he told them he'd sue them if they included him again.

They never did.

"When do you have to go back to work?" he asked, worried about her state of mind at the moment. Hopefully it wasn't too soon.

She licked her lips and stared at him. "I haven't decided. Maybe a few weeks? I have to make a decision about this place, and get it all sorted," she said. "Work out what I'm doing with all this." Her arms went up, indicating the mess around them. "It's going to be so very hard," she said quietly.

Braxton took her in his arms again. A peacefulness came over him. Time had not lessened his feelings for Sierra. This felt right, so very right, but he couldn't let himself fall in love with her all over again when she would be leaving town in a few weeks time.

And leave him, once more, to mourn.

Chapter Five

Braxton convinced Sierra to join him and a group of other riders for one of his more laid-back trail rides he'd been conducting that morning.

The groups usually consisted more of tourists than anyone, but occasionally they were joined by people who hadn't ridden for some years and wanted to get back into it.

Like Sierra.

She'd found her old riding gear in one of the packing boxes at Evelyn's place. The boots still fitted, but not much else, so today she wore tight jeans and a pink shirt that accentuated her curvy body.

He'd had to stop himself staring on more than one occasion.

Finally, they were alone.

All the horses had been brushed, fed, and were now resting.

They sat on the porch of Braxton's ranch house eating lunch. A hastily put together lunch of sandwiches and coffee.

"How did it feel to be back in the saddle?" He stared at her over his coffee mug.

She wriggled about in her seat. "The backside is a bit tender, but not too bad. I did enjoy it though." She brushed her wayward hair out of her face and took another bite of her sandwich. "I don't suppose you have time for another ride later?"

His heart thudded in his chest. Time alone with Sierra – it was what he wanted, and yet, perhaps he shouldn't...

He closed his eyes momentarily, then opened them to find her staring at him.

"If you're serious, I'll make it happen," he said. "I have workers for a reason – to take the load off."

"Look, if you don't want to,"

He cut her off. "I do, of course I do. It's just..." How did he say it? "I still have feelings for you, Sierra. But,"

"But I'm going back to the city, right?" She looked down into her lap. She'd voiced exactly what he was feeling.

"I've tried to tell myself that's not it at all, but I know deep in my heart, it is." He felt like a jerk. He had feelings for the woman sitting in front of him. Strong and genuine feelings that wouldn't go away.

He didn't know what to do about it.

"We can still be friends, right? I don't have a choice, Brax," she said, staring into her lap again. "I have to return to work after my leave is up. I'm just not sure when that will be."

At least she was being honest with him. "I understand," he said quietly. "In the meantime, we can still hang out, right? On the understanding it can't go anywhere, so it's friends only."

"Sure." She didn't sound so sure, or happy, but it would have to do. They had no other choice.

* * *

Sierra sat astride Storm, one of Braxton's *quieter* horses.

They'd finished lunch, caught up on each other's lives, and decided to go for a ride around his property.

"We have a missing mare," he said. "A very pregnant mare. We can look out for her while we're out and about. It will be double-duty – I hope you don't mind."

"Not at all. It's so long since I've been out here, I know I'll enjoy it."

He finished packing the bottles of water and some snacks into a saddlebag and mounted his horse, Amos. He attached the satellite phone to his belt and prepared to leave. "Ready?"

She took a deep breath. "Ready as I'll ever be." She smiled tentatively and Braxton's radar went up - she was having seconds thoughts. "You don't have to come with me," he said. "Honestly. Don't feel bad if you don't want to go."

She wriggled about in the saddle. "No, it's fine. I want to spend time with you while I can, and I don't mind riding. I've missed it."

He nodded then flicked the reins and Amos moved forward. Storm followed.

They hadn't been riding long when Sierra took off. "Race you to the end of the paddock," she yelled over her shoulder.

Did she forget how big his property was?

She was gone before he could answer. He watched as the wind blew her hair up, sending it flapping through the air.

He'd missed this. Missed them riding together. He finally caught up to her as she slowed down. "Over there, Brax," she said, pointing across the paddock. "Is that your missing mare?"

He followed her hand and squinted. He couldn't make it out from this distance but was hopeful it was.

He turned Amos around and headed to the area she'd indicated.

"Dammit," he said under his breath. It was indeed his missing mare, and she was in labor. This was exactly why he liked to patrol the area on a regular basis.

He checked her over carefully. Her breathing was labored, and she was having trouble giving birth. He pulled out the satellite phone and called Jeff Johnson, the vet he used regularly. Then he called Austin who would bring some equipment to help the mare while they waited for the vet to arrive.

He stroked the back of her neck. "It will be alright," he said softly, trying to calm her. The mare whinnied as her eyes opened wide, terrified.

He sat there patiently continuing to talk softly to the mare, waiting for help to arrive. Sierra joined him. "Will she be alright," she asked.

"I hope so, but they can't be too much longer. She's not in a good way."

Austin arrived not long after, and Braxton began to check the mare over. He donned some gloves, deciding he couldn't wait for the vet any longer. Two hooves had made their way out of the birth canal but seemed to be stuck.

Austin sat by the mare, taking over where Braxton had left off – trying to calm her. Braxton pushed his arms up inside her and pulled.

It wasn't working. He sat back on ground, giving the mare a rest for awhile, then tried again. Still nothing. He continued this process until the mare was too exhausted to continue.

Finally, the vet arrived and took over.

"It's a breech," he announced. "No wonder she's having trouble. And you."

He donned his long rubber gloves, adding a lubricant, then reached inside the mare, feeling for the foal's other legs.

Normally she would heave and kick at this sort of intrusion, but as Braxton found out earlier, she was too exhausted for any of that.

"Ah!" Finally, the vet located the foal's legs, and pulled – gently at first, but when that didn't work, he pulled with all his might.

Slowly but surely, he pulled the foal out of its mother, then softly laid him on the blanket Austin had laid out.

Braxton was extremely relieved; he was certain they were going to lose this foal.

Sierra stood shoulder to shoulder with him, waiting for the foal to stand. But he didn't. He was too exhausted.

"Is he okay, doc?" Braxton asked, feeling quite worried for the new foal. Not to mention its mother.

"I don't know yet. Give him a minute or two." Jeff was pulling off his gloves as he watched the foal. Braxton knew what came next. If he didn't get up by himself soon, he would need intervention.

As he shuffled about, then began to stand by himself, albeit wobbly, everyone let out the breath they'd been holding. Braxton turned to see tears streaming down Sierra's face.

"That's the most amazing thing I've ever seen," she said.

He reached out and wiped the tears from her cheek. "Yeah, it is pretty amazing," he said, pulling her into his arms.

He had to admit to himself that having her in his arms was his favorite thing to do.

What happened to their friends-only deal?

He told himself he was comforting an old friend, but he knew it went well beyond that.

He was falling for Sierra all over again.

* * *

"What an amazing day," Sierra said, when they arrived back at the ranch some hours after they'd set out.

Austin had left them only to return later with a horse float. They needed to get the wandering mare to safety, along with her baby.

The pair had sat with mother and baby until she was safely on her way home, and finally they were back, both famished.

"I don't know about you," Braxton said, climbing down from his horse. "But I'm starving."

Sierra attempted to climb down on her own and nearly fell. Braxton quickly grabbed her, avoiding a disaster.

"Easy," he said, coming up behind her and guiding her to solid ground. Her lingering perfume got into his nostrils, and the fragrance reminded him of decades ago when they'd snuggled up on her grandmother's couch.

He nuzzled her neck. It felt good. She felt good.

"Brax... we had a deal, right?"

Shaken, he pulled back suddenly. "Not that I'm complaining," she said. "But it will be hard for us both when it's all over."

He grabbed the reins and led Amos into the stables. Sierra followed behind with Storm. "I know. And I'm sorry. It won't happen again."

He made a silent commitment to them both to ensure it didn't happen again, but could he trust himself?

He wasn't certain he could.

After brushing down the horses and seeing them back in their stalls and fed, they returned to the ranch house.

"I'm a mess, I need to have a shower," he said, pulling down a mug from the cupboard, and filling the kettle with water. "Make yourself a coffee, tea, or whatever it is you want. I won't be too long."

She nodded, and he felt her gaze burn a hole in his back as he walked away. Man, this was hard. Much more difficult than he'd anticipated, but they both had to abstain, or it would be history repeating itself.

They'd both be miserable when they had to separate once more. Even after all this time.

* * *

H e already felt better. Standing under that cool shower made all his troubles wash away. Not the least of them being the lost mare.

At least now he knew she was safe and well.

But what do to about Sierra? Man, he was head over heels for her. Again.

He washed himself as he pondered this problem. It wasn't as though he could ignore her. They'd been friends too long for that.

She'd also made it clear she didn't want to get involved. *So what was the problem?* The problem was, Sierra would leave him again.

Okay, so she wouldn't leave him per say, but she would leave town to go back to work. In the big city, which was hours away.

He leaned back against the shower stall. He felt totally deflated. He should never have let himself get close to her again – he was asking for trouble, and he knew it.

Even way back when they were dating, he knew she was special. It's why he hadn't been able to get her out of his head all these years.

Why the hell didn't he ring her? Or storm into her workplace and demand she leave?

Because that wasn't him. She had to make her own decisions, and that was the decision she'd made.

If only he could convince her to stay this time, but she'd already made up her mind. She was going back to work in less than three weeks.

She'd only come back for Evelyn's funeral, and to sort out her property.

He turned the water to cool before stepping out, as he always did. It was then he heard a scream. Sierra was in trouble!

He turned off the water and grabbed a towel. Draping it around himself he ran to the kitchen where he'd left her.

He was panicking and out of breath by the time he arrived.

She was cringing in the corner of the room. "What's happened? Are you okay?" He went to her, but she couldn't speak, she was too frightened. "Just point" he said.

"A spider? You're scared of a little spider?" He laughed and she grimaced.

She slowly got up from the floor. "It isn't a *little* spider," she said quietly. "It's huge."

"You lived in the outback most of your life, and still scared of spiders." He shook his head and scooped up the offending creature, taking it outside. "I need to get dressed, and then I'll be back."

He walked away still shaking his head in disbelief.

It wasn't long before he reappeared, fully clothed. "Ready to go out to dinner?"

She stared at him. "I thought we were eating here? Never mind," she said, shaking her head.

Eating in presented too much temptation. They'd be in a confined space together, and that might not end well.

Okay, so it probably would from his perspective, until it came time for them to separate again in a few weeks time.

"There's a newish restaurant in town, *Angel's Kitchen*, have you been there?" He hadn't eaten out forever. No point going alone.

She shook her head. "I haven't really had time, with everything else going on."

He guessed she meant the funeral and such. Plus she'd been staying with Mel, and likely eating there too. "If you're happy with that, we'll head on over."

She agreed, and they were soon on their way.

* * *

Good old-fashioned meals. That's what they had at *Angel's Kitchen*. He'd have to keep that in mind. Might be worth popping in now and again.

If Sierra was able to accompany him, even better.

Angel turned out to be a 70-year-old grandmother named Joyce Kingston, who had retired but quickly become bored.

Braxton found it quite amusing. But thinking about it, Angel's Kitchen had a better ring to it than Grandma's Kitchen or Joyce's Kitchen.

He ordered the beef stew, and Sierra followed suit. It was the best meal he'd had for months. "The food is fantastic, Angel. Er, Joyce," he said with a grin. "I'll definitely be coming back."

"What about you, honey," the older woman asked.

Sierra stared at him and licked her lips. "I'm leaving town in a few weeks," she said. "But I'll make the effort to come back before I go."

"I'll get her back before then," Braxton said. "Your food is delicious."

She handed him the dessert menu. "Go your hardest, sonny," she said with a grin, then walked away.

Sierra looked at him over the top of the menu. "Any recommendations," she asked.

"It all looks good," he said. "This place is a great find. I'll definitely keep it in mind."

It wasn't long before Joyce was back to take their orders. "What'll you have, sonny?"

Braxton grinned at Sierra, then looked to their host. "The apple pie sounds fantastic. I'll have that."

"Made with my own two hands, sonny. What about you," she asked Sierra.

"Same, thanks."

She returned a short time later with their desserts, and two coffees. "Drinks on the house for first-time visitors," she announced, and disappeared again.

They tucked into their desserts and sat sipping their complimentary coffee. "I had a wonderful day, Brax," Sierra told him.

He reached across the table and covered her hand with his own.

She stared at their entwined hands. "Brax," she warned. "Friends, remember?"

He grimaced and chose his words carefully. "Is there any chance you might stay after all?" His heart raced while he waited for her to respond.

"None at all. I have a job to go back too."

He quickly pulled his hand away. "I know," he said. "I just hoped you'd changed your mind." He leaned back in his chair.

"I can spare a few hours tomorrow if you want to sort out your grandmother's place a bit more?"

She jumped at the chance. "That would be fabulous. Thanks so much for the offer, Brax."

Braxton knew the next few weeks were going to be hard, really hard, but what could he do? They led totally separate lives, and there was no point getting too cozy together when fate was going to tear them apart. And in the not too distance future.

Chapter Six

Sierra had thoroughly enjoyed herself yesterday with Braxton, and wished there could be many more like it.

It had been a day of firsts for her – first time watching a horse being born, first time alone with Braxton in his house, and first time seeing his very bare, very muscled arms and chest.

She needed to get the latter out of her mind, and quickly.

She was not going to let herself fall for him all over again. She was not!

Try as she might, she had to admit it was already too late. In all these years she hadn't been able to totally eradicate thoughts of him from her mind.

She mentally shook herself; he was still there, still weaving his magic over her.

Ten years. They'd been separated by distance for ten years, but she knew he was still *the one*. She'd dated plenty of men over that time, but they never lasted more than three dates. No one ever lived up to her standards of what she expected from her dates. From potential partners.

Braxton had spoiled her all those years ago. Spoiled her for other men. He was more man than she ever wanted.

When he'd ran into that kitchen to protect her, her heart fluttered. Okay, so it was only a spider he was *protecting* her from, but he was there for her.

He'd always been there for her.

She'd needed him the day of the funeral, and he'd come through. He'd gone with her to Gran's house for support, too. Looking back, he'd always been there, when no one else had, except for Gran of course.

Braxton was just Brax, always knowing what she needed, and when she needed it.

Her stomach did a flip-flop. It felt like there were a bunch of butterflies fluttering around in there.

She put her hands to her stomach and looked down. *What would it be like to have Braxton's baby growing inside her?*

She shook that thought away. She was leaving in less than three weeks. She had no time for fanciful thoughts such as babies. Her career had always taken precedence over all else.

Besides, Braxton had never voiced his wish for babies. Or if he had, he'd not made her privy to those thoughts.

She studied herself in the hallway mirror, Gran's beloved full-length mirror, then like a wistful teenager, shoved a pillow up her shirt. Her body clock was ticking, but she wasn't willing to have just anyone's baby. It was Braxton's or none.

She pulled the pillow out and again stared at her reflection. "What the heck are you going to do, Sierra West?" she asked. "You can't have it all. Make a choice, Braxton or a career?"

She shook her head and walked away, shoulders slumped. If she could have both she'd be happy. But in her heart of hearts, she knew that wasn't true. All she really wanted was Braxton. Her first love, and if she got her way, her last.

* * *

"You didn't hear a word I said, did you?" Austin's voice broke through Braxton's thoughts.

He looked down from his horse, at the intrusion to his very private memories.

Thoughts of Sierra kept flooding his mind to the point he couldn't concentrate on work. He'd done the exact same thing when she left ten years ago. His mind had drifted off to places it shouldn't drift.

To holding her, kissing her, and just being with her.

Austin interrupted his wayward thoughts once more. "Boss," he said a little more loudly. "We've got another mare gone AWOL. There has to be a broken fence somewhere."

This time he was on full alert. "Round up a few of the boys to come with me. We'll go check it out."

He turned Amos around and headed for the ranch house to get some supplies while the other farm hands saddled their horses. "Tell them to meet me at the ranch."

Losing a mare broke Braxton's heart. The animals he bred were worth money to him, he admitted that, but he hated to see any of his animal family in pain or suffering.

It had cut him to the gut the other day when he thought he was about to lose both mother and baby. Standing by, watching the mare suffer, was almost more than he could bear. Thankfully it had turned out well, no small thanks to his wonderful veterinarian.

He was grateful Sierra had been able to share the experience of a new life with him. He got to do it on a regular basis, but it was totally new for her.

The look of utter joy on her face was almost more than he could bear. The look of love. It was the same look he'd seen all those years ago, when they dated, and she looked at him.

He prayed he would get to see it again and wondered if there was a way to convince her to stay. If he could coax her to stay for a few more weeks, he might persuade her to stay forever.

At least he hoped he could.

If he couldn't do that, then there was no chance for them.

Braxton did a final check of his supplies, then handed out water and snacks to all the men, who had assembled at the ranch.

They would bring the tools and equipment for any necessary repairs.

He checked the satellite phone was fully charged and clipped it onto his belt.

He couldn't afford to be without it. It could have been a catastrophe for that mare if he hadn't been prepared.

Tightening the cinch, he glanced up to check if the others were ready to leave. They were.

He needed to get his mind back on the job, because his work was important. If the missing mare got out, it could mean her demise. Beyond his property was barren land. She would not survive out there alone.

Mounting Amos, he joined the men and they set out. He was determined to sort things out with Sierra but forced himself to put her to the back of his mind for the next few hours.

He knew that was going to be a tall order.

"Over here, Boss." One of the workers called back over his shoulder after they'd been riding for some time. Braxton jumped from his mount.

The worker pulled wire and pliers from his saddlebag and immediately got to work on the hole in the fence.

The other men rode the length of the fence checking for other breaks but found none. Braxton sat atop Amos and looked about, trying to spot the mare, but had no joy.

One thing was certain, as far as he could tell, she hadn't left the property. She was nowhere to be seen outside his property line.

"Check over there, Charlie" he instructed one of his men. "Take Frank with you." There was a small hill in the distance, and it was impossible to see beyond it.

As they disappeared into the valley, Braxton held his breath, wondering what they were going to find. Hopefully not a dead mare.

He nearly hadn't ridden out here today but had to get his mind off Sierra and back on the job. It almost worked.

When he had nothing to do, his mind drifted to the blonde beauty he wanted to be more than his friend.

He felt certain she felt the same way too, but they were going in different directions. He had his property to run and wanted to stay in the outback. Sierra had her high-powered job in the city, managing one of the largest hotels in the state.

They were more than five hours apart – a long-term relationship was not possible. It wouldn't work for either of them.

The more he thought about it, the bigger the headache. And the headache was becoming more like a migraine, the more he thought about their dilemma.

He glanced up to see one of the workers waving at him to join them. Braxton flicked the reins and rode toward them.

As he rode over the hill, he spotted the mare. She looked to be fine, which was a relief.

Charlie hooked a rope around her neck and led her back to the rest of the group.

The worry of the mare off his mind, he went back to thinking about Sierra and their future.

What was he going to do if she didn't stay? His heart was already shattering.

***

Bent over a dusty box, Sierra blew her hair out of her face.

She'd been at it for hours, endeavoring to sort out Gran's possessions. It was heart wrenching; her grandmother's life had been reduced to a few dozen boxes. And now, here she was, contemplating what to do with Evelyn's treasured possessions.

Gran had seen the end coming and instructed Sierra to throw out what she deemed to be rubbish, and donate the rest. A handful of heirlooms and much-loved pieces had already been sorted and put aside for Sierra, long before her frail grandmother had left her decades-long home.

She straightened up, brushing aside the dust and the wayward tears. She knew it would be hard but had no idea it would be this difficult.

Equally tough was deciding about her future. There weren't many options available to her. Being a small town with few employment opportunities, and none in her line of work, she would eventually have to leave.

Not only would she be leaving this beautiful house behind, but also Braxton. Her heart ached, and she hadn't even left yet.

Her head snapped up at the banging on the door. "Sierra? It's Brax." His voice was loud and strong, and she wondered what he wanted.

She opened the door and stared into his face. It was a welcome relief. "Hey Brax."

He reached out and brushed his hand across her face. "You're covered in dust." He stared into her face. "You have tear streaks. Are you okay," he asked as he shoved the stray hair back behind her ear.

She ignored the question.

"You really look a mess," he said, laughing as he pushed his way into the house.

"Why don't you come in?" Sierra said sarcastically as he strolled inside.

He chuckled and looked around, then whistled low. "It's a bit of a mess," he said. "What have you decided to do?"

She looked to the floor. "Honestly? I can't decide. I really don't want to sell this beautiful place. Gran loved it so much, and so do I."

Braxton wandered about, then began to climb the spiral staircase.

"I know your old bedroom is up here, but what else? It's so long since I've been up here, and I can't recall."

Sierra followed behind. "Mostly bedrooms, but a couple of bathrooms," she said. Her interest was piqued. "What are you thinking?"

He reached the top of the stairs and stopped, glancing about. "Not sure yet. Give me time."

She waited at the top of the staircase and studied him as he scurried from room to room.

"This was your room, right?" he called back over his shoulder.

She stood frozen to the spot and swallowed. This was so much harder than she'd expected. "Yes," she said softly. So quietly she was convinced Brax wouldn't be able to hear her response.

By this time, he'd entered the room, but popped his head around the corner. "Are you okay," he asked as he approached her.

His arms went up as though he was about to hug her, to comfort her. She shook her head vigorously. If she let him in, there would be a waterfall of tears. Once she started, she wouldn't stop.

The time since Gran's death had left her emotionally drained.

She had to be strong. Had to get this place sorted and leave. She had less than three weeks to achieve that goal, but she was determined to make it happen.

She ducked back down the stairs and felt more than a little guilty when she looked up to see the hurt expression on his face.

By the time he joined her again, she had sat herself on a sheet-covered chair. At least she wouldn't have to clean the furniture before disposing of it.

"Sierra, I..." he began to speak but she stopped him.

She shook her head again. "We can't do this. *I* can't do this," she said. "I'll be gone again before we know it, and we'll both be left with broken hearts."

He settled himself close to her, then fidgeted with his hands. He suddenly turned his head and stared into her eyes. "What if there was a way for you to stay?"

Her heartbeat accelerated, and her belly fluttered. *Was it possible? Could Brax make that happen?*

Moments after the excitement of possibility, she felt the thud of disappointment.

He'd seen the disappointment on her face, she couldn't hide it. He reached over and covered her hands with his own. "What do you do for a living," he asked gently.

He knew – they'd discussed it only days ago. She looked at him quizzically. "I manage a big hotel in the city. You know that. But what does that..."

He interrupted her. "You said you wanted to keep this place, and rightly so. It's a beautiful piece of history. Your history, and the town's history." He squeezed her hand reassuringly.

She nodded.

"Have you thought of turning it into a B&B? A bed and breakfast. Or a small hotel. You've got the credentials, the expertise. You could make a go of it."

She felt light-headed with happiness. Why hadn't *she* thought of it? She knew the answer almost before she asked herself the question. She'd been consumed by grief at the loss of her sweet grandmother, as well as by guilt at not spending as much time with Gran as she wanted.

There were so many regrets troubling her, not the least being working and living so far away.

"Do you think it's possible?" she asked softly, suddenly standing and gazing about the room. "I mean, right now it's a horrible mess." She suddenly felt giddy with excitement.

Brax stood and put his arm around her. "You'd need to get someone in to access the place before you could make any solid decisions," he said. "Each room may need to have its own private bathroom, I'm not sure."

She nodded, barely taking it all in. All she could think was this was a way to keep Gran's place and stay home. This home - Oakdale. The place she'd grown up in and loved more than life itself.

She never had, and never would consider her tiny unit in the city to be home, despite having lived there for over a decade.

Sierra straightened her shoulders and stood tall. "Let's do it," she said confidently. Much more confidently than she felt.

* * *

The house was a buzz of activity.

Together they'd sought out an architect, who had his own regular builder. The pair were upstairs right now doing their first walk-though.

They were both busy jotting down notes and taking photographs. Until they finished their surveillance, everything was still up in the air.

Sierra sat nervously downstairs, butted up close to Braxton.

He put his hand over hers, trying to calm her. She looked up toward the mezzanine, straining to hear.

She watched the men scurrying from room to room, measuring tapes in their hands. Braxton was pretty sure they could make this happen, but the cost was an unknown entity.

Sierra might not want to go to all that expense.

What seemed like a lifetime, but in reality, was only an hour or so, the two men reappeared. Both held notebooks in their hands and appeared to be studying them.

"It's possible," the architect suddenly said, startling Sierra. "I'll do the drawings, then confer with our builder here," He indicated the man standing next to him. "Then I'll get back to you. It will take a few days at least."

His outstretched hand was the first indication the conversation was over.

"I'll call you when I'm done," he said, handing her a business card. "You have a beautiful place here," he said. "It would be a shame to see it go to waste."

Before they knew it, the two men were gone.

"Phew, that was intense, and he gave nothing away," Braxton said. He watched as Sierra let out the breath she was holding. "Now we wait for the results."

Sierra stood, scrutinizing the room. "I can picture it now. This would make a wonderful guest lounge." She indicated the room they were currently in. "The kitchen would need to be renovated, especially if I decided to have the option of chef prepared meals."

He followed her as she flounced out to the kitchen. "It is a bit, shall we say, drab?" It had definitely seen better days. "Even if you sold the place, you'd probably need to update the kitchen first."

She nodded. "You're right, of course. No one would buy this place as is. It hasn't been painted or renovated in decades. Gran loved it as it was." Her voice cracked as she spoke.

He moved toward her and pulled her close, putting his arm around her shoulders. "I know," he said softly. "It's an amazing house. But either way, it needs updating now."

"Yeah, I know," she said equally quietly.

She followed him to the large entrance hall. "This," he said pointing to a spot on the side. "This could be your reception desk."

He could picture it all in his head, and was certain she could too, working in that industry.

"It would have to be era appropriate," she said excitedly, almost bursting at the seams.

He grinned. She was finally warming to his idea.

Now all that needed to happen was have the costs within her financial reach.

"I'm exhausted," she said. "Not that I've done much, but this is all mentally draining."

He totally understood. He was heading that way too. He'd done very little on his property since Sierra came back, relying instead on his workers. They were all more than capable of continuing without him for a few days while he helped her.

Austin had been with him from the very beginning, and he'd left him in charge. Besides, if anything urgent came up, Austin would call him.

"Let's go for a walk, then coffee," Braxton suggested. "Then we'll come back and sort out more of Evelyn's stuff."

It broke his heart each time he mentioned Evelyn. Sierra seemed to grieve a little more every time she was mentioned.

"Sure," she said, grabbing his hand and heading for the front door. "We both need a break."

It felt like each time they were together, they became a little closer. It was reminiscent of their teenage years, only they weren't teenagers any more. And this wasn't just until they'd had enough of each other.

If Braxton had his way, this would be their forever. But he still wasn't convinced any of it would happen. It took an awful lot of money to make major renovations to any place, let alone an old building such as this one.

He was more than willing to lend Sierra a substantial amount of money to see this through, but would she accept his offer?

It felt as though his heart died a little just thinking about it. No matter what, he would put on a brave face, and wondered whether Sierra felt the same way he did.

If she did, it certainly wasn't showing.

Chapter Seven

It had been an excruciating few days waiting for the architect's report.

They sat together going over it. They were yet to look at the bottom line – the cost.

Sierra sat stiffly, leaning forward on the chair with Braxton close beside her.

He could see she was eager with anticipation but terrified at the same time. Together they read the suggestions – give each bedroom its own ensuite bathroom, making the accommodation more appealing.

Both existing bathrooms were extremely large, so they could also be turned into private rooms with their own ensuite, giving the house an additional two rooms to rent out. These would be much larger rooms and could become the wedding or executive suites.

Sierra had called and asked the architect to add a new kitchen into the quote. He'd visited a couple of days earlier, again with his builder, so they could incorporate it into the same quote.

They both thoroughly read the report. They scanned over the drawings of the changes, then looked at each other enthusiastically.

Braxton reached over and brushed some stray hair behind her ear. "Are you ready?" he asked, referring to turning the page to see the dollar figure.

She nodded. "I think so," she said quietly, her voice breaking from anticipation.

He leaned back. "Before I do," he said, sucking in a big breath. "I want you to know I'm willing to lend you whatever you need."

She waved a hand in the air. "Thanks, Brax, but I don't need your money. If it's that much, I won't do it." Disappointed flittered across her pretty face.

"We'll talk more later."

He turned the page and his eyes skipped the summary of expenses, down to the bottom of the page with the final figure.

It was big, a little more than he'd anticipated, but not a lot. Overall, it was reasonable. He hoped Sierra thought so too.

He glanced across at her, trying to gauge her reaction. She simply sat staring.

His heart thumped. She wasn't going to go ahead. She looked... he wasn't sure what she looked, but it wasn't happy.

He sat back against the sofa. All his plans for their future together suddenly fell in a heap. She was going to leave here in three weeks, and he'd never see her again.

He felt lightheaded with disappointment, with the sheer horror of it all. He couldn't begin to contemplate his life without Sierra. He'd spent the past ten years trying to get her out of his head. It didn't work, had never worked. He didn't want to go through that again.

Ever.

He licked his lips – his mouth had gone so dry. His heart was pumping so fast, he felt giddy.

"So... what do you think?" He tried to sound normal but didn't recognize his own voice. Would she notice?

Her head shot around to face him.

He wondered if she felt the same way as he did.

"I," She looked down to the figure once more. "It's doable," she said softly. "My unit in the city is worth way more than this. And I have some savings – you don't spend much when you're working sixty hours or more every week."

His heart soared. *She was staying! She would be here for the rest of her life.*

"I can't believe it! You're staying." His breath came out in a whoosh.

Now she looked annoyed. "I didn't say that," she said sharply. "I didn't once say I'd stay here if I turned this into accommodation."

What was she saying? Did he misinterpret everything she'd said, the way she'd acted toward him?

"I could easily install someone here as manager," she said quietly.

His heart shattered all over again. It was *deja vu* from ten years ago.

"So you're leaving after all," he asked quietly, his voice cracking. This was not how it was meant to be.

"I didn't say that either," she snapped. "I need to take this all in and crunch some figures. Then and only then will I make a decision."

Why did she go through the process of getting an architect to do the report if she had no intention of staying and running it herself?

He felt as though he'd been sucker punched. He sat in stunned silence until Sierra's voice broke through the fog.

"Brax, are you okay?" Her voice seemed a thousand miles away.

He shoved his fingers through his hair and nodded. "Yeah, sure. I just thought..." He stared into her face. The beautiful face he loved so much. "It doesn't matter what I thought. I need to go. Catch you later."

He kissed her forehead, then left before things got too intense.

* * *

Sierra had been trying to work out the sums in her head when Brax broke into her thoughts.

He'd taken her off-guard when he'd blurted out about her staying. Sure, that was her intention, but until she crunched those numbers, she couldn't say for sure if she'd go ahead.

She also needed to make some calls and find out how much she could feasibly charge guests to stay here.

There were a few other motels within a reasonable distance of town, but none here. She hoped Oakdale, their unique town, and the beautiful old building would be a big drawcard.

Tourists came here all the time, just to see their amazing old buildings. But would they be willing to stay overnight? Or to eat at her hotel if she went ahead?

They were the million-dollar questions.

Brax made it sound so simple. He had no idea, but she did. The last ten years had been spent studying the hospitality industry, going to university and studying. She'd worked her way up the corporate ladder until she'd become the best in her industry and managing one of the largest hotels in the state, if not the country.

She'd not only met with every day tourists but had dealt with some of the biggest celebrities in the world. Personally taking care of their specific needs – because that's what you did to keep your guests happy.

There was so much more involved than just renovating a building and opening the doors.

She sucked in a cleansing breath, then let it whoosh out again.

Sierra found a notebook in one of Gran's drawers, and sat down with her calculator and pen and started crunching those numbers.

When she'd done that, she made those phone calls, pretending to be potential customers looking for a room.

She'd called the local Manchester store to get a quote on linen, pillows, and towels, then did some more number crunching.

She'd need to have curtains or blinds custom made, so that would be another expense she'd need to include, once she organized that extra expense.

She called a well-known real estate agent in the city to get a tentative quote on what her unit was worth and checked the balance of her bank account.

She would also have to factor in staff costs, because even if she did stay, she couldn't do it all alone. If she didn't say, that was even more expense for staffing.

Before she knew it, darkness was beginning to set in. She was near exhaustion and knew she had to call it a day.

She picked up her cell phone and dialed. "Brax, have you eaten yet? I'm starving."

* * *

When he'd walked out, he was sure it was the end for them.

He'd glanced across as he opened the door and saw the hurt look on her face. He did that to her. *How could he? How could he hurt the woman he loved?*

He felt like a heel. He hadn't meant to do it, but he'd felt hurt himself. He hadn't considered what she'd been going through at that moment. Or how she would be feeling.

He'd only been thinking of himself. What a jerk he'd been!

Somehow, he had to make it up to her. He'd considered calling and inviting her out to dinner, but she was probably too mad at him.

And he wouldn't blame her, not one little bit.

His cell phone rang. "What?" he screeched into the phone, madder at himself than anyone else.

"Well hello to you too, dear cousin."

Mel. That's all he needed right now. "Yeah." He didn't want to talk to Mel. She'd just increase his blood pressure more.

"I just wanted to make sure you're still okay for Saturday night."

He sighed. As if he'd forget – Mel wouldn't let him. "Saturday night? What's on Saturday night?" He knew damned well what she was talking about, but if he was annoyed, he was damned sure she would be too.

"Braxton!" she screeched down the line. "You better been there – the flyers..." She stopped cold.

He frowned. Now he knew she was up to something and wondered again what it was. "Flyers, huh?"

"Uh, no. You must have misunderstood." She suddenly went quiet.

No, he didn't. He was one thousand percent certain of it.

She rattled on for another twenty minutes about nothing, reiterating his availability on Saturday night before hanging up.

Flyers, eh? If he could find them, he might get to the bottom of Mel's scheme.

He'd just settled back down when his cell rang again. "What now?" He practically screamed down the line. He'd had more than enough of Mel's antics for one night.

"Is it a bad time?" Sierra's gentle voice carried over the line. Now he really felt like a jerk.

He sat up straight and answered as calmly as he could. Not that he was mad at Sierra; Mel was the one who deserved his wrath right now. "Sorry, I've just had a bit of a run-in with Mel."

The line was silent.

"I'm sorry about before," he said quickly. "It's not your fault I assumed."

But it was certainly *his* fault. He thought if he could find a way for her to stay, she *would* stay. He should have asked her what *she* wanted, and not gone on what *he* wanted.

"Have you eaten," she asked, totally ignoring his statement. "I'm famished."

"*Angel's Kitchen* or somewhere else?" he asked, grabbing his hat on the way out the door as they continued to chat.

"Sounds great," she said. "Meet you there?"

"You're on."

He disconnected the call and whistled as he strolled toward his truck.

Joyce, the owner of *Angel's Kitchen*, guided them toward a secluded booth in the back corner. "You love-birds check out the menu, and I'll be back."

Braxton couldn't help but grin. He didn't generally like it when people assumed, but in this case, he had no problem with it.

Sierra raised her eyebrows at him. "Love-birds, eh? And I see you didn't correct her."

He slid a hand across the table to cover hers. "I'm sorry about earlier," he said, apologizing once again. "I'll try not to be such a jerk in future."

He couldn't help himself – he grinned again.

"You look really sorry, too," she admonished him. "But you're hard to stay mad at." She smiled.

He'd missed that too.

He squeezed her hand. He'd really missed their easy banter and touching her. He'd always loved to touch her; it gave him such a thrill.

Joyce brought over a jug of water and two glasses, then filled each glass. "You two look really cozy together," she said. "Like you were made for each other."

She winked at him then slinked away. "I'll come back later, when you've had a chance to check the menu."

"Everything looks great," Sierra said, peeking over the top of the menu. "If last time is anything to go by, it will all be delicious."

They made their decisions, and Joyce suddenly reappeared. "What are you having?" she asked Sierra, then wrote down her order. "What about you, Sonny? You look like a steak and fries kinda man."

He was indeed, and he couldn't help but smile. Sierra chuckled.

"You two were in here last week, if I recall?"

"We were," Braxton said. "The food was so delicious we decided to come back." He extended his hand. "Braxton Chalmers, and this is Sierra West."

"West? You any relation to Evelyn West?"

"My grandmother, but she was more like a mother. Brought me up. I've come back to sort out her affairs."

Joyce nodded solemnly. "She was a great woman. I'm sorry for your loss," she said warmly. "What's happening with the house? Is it going up for sale?"

Sierra glanced across at Braxton. "I'm not sure yet. I'm trying to find a way to keep it in the family."

Joyce leaned in and hugged Sierra. "I'm glad," she whispered. "Evelyn would have wanted that."

Moments later she was gone, and Sierra stared after her.

Suddenly she was all business. "After you left, I spent hours crunching numbers and making phone calls," Sierra said, looking down at her hands and avoiding his eyes at all cost.

He didn't want to ask the question for fear of upsetting her, but he couldn't stand the wait. "Have you come to a decision?"

Her eyes met his.

"First of all, I need to tell you something. Don't take it the wrong way." She looked down at her hands again.

His heart thudded in his chest. *She was leaving. Or she was leaving him.* Either one was catastrophic to him.

"Whatever I do, it has to be a business decision. Making business choices based on the heart never work out."

He nodded, terrified to say a word in case it influenced her.

"I honestly don't want the house to leave my family's hands. And as you know, I'm the only family Gran had left, so that means it's up to me to do everything in my power to keep the house."

He nodded again, his heart pounding endlessly, waiting for the bottom line. *Was she renovating, or selling up?*

"There are still a few things I need to look into, but I'm hoping to keep the house." She smiled tentatively.

Her words didn't serve to ease his fears. She still didn't make a commitment to stay, only to keep the house. Maybe.

As she'd pointed out this afternoon, she could easily renovate the house and turn it into a hotel, then employ a manager to run it.

When he'd come up with the idea, he was certain it was going to ensure she stayed. As much as he loved that old house, he didn't care whether Sierra kept it or not. Not really.

What he did care about was her staying in town and eventually becoming his wife.

He wanted her to have his children, and he wanted to grow old with her.

His wayward thoughts were interrupted by Joyce returning to their table. "I was trying to place your name. You own that horse property outside town, don't you?"

He frowned. "Sure do. *Whispering Pines.* How did you know?"

"My brother's boy, he does a few odd jobs for you."

Now his interest was piqued. "A few odd jobs? I don't have anyone doing odd jobs as far as

I know." He grinned. He personally hired every person who worked for him. In all these years, he'd not had to fire even one of them.

"His name is Austin Addison. Do you know him?"

Braxton laughed out loud. "Austin has been with me for years. But he doesn't do odd jobs – he's my Property Manager and does a damned fine job too."

She grinned. "Oh," she said. "Eat up before it gets cold. We'll talk sometime."

"That's hilarious," he told Sierra when the older woman was out of ear-shot, then tucked into his dinner.

* * *

They'd had a wonderful night together, at least he did. He'd thoroughly enjoyed his evening with Sierra, despite knowing in the back of his mind she could be leaving in a matter of weeks.

He hadn't brought up the subject of Evelyn's house again, because he didn't want to spoil their time together.

After they'd left the restaurant, he'd taken her to *The Lookout*, which overlooked the town below.

It had been more than a decade since she'd been up there and said she was keen to see it again. He didn't want to think that it might be the last time she saw it for another decade or even more.

As they sat in his truck, he reached across and put an arm around her.

"This is nice," she said, resting her head and staring at the town of Oakdale below. The entire town was lit up by the moonlight, but they could also see the light streaming out of the windows of the houses.

He pulled her a little closer. "It is that," he said, squeezing her shoulder. "I really missed this, but I missed you more," he said leaning in closer to kiss her.

She turned toward him and had to have seen him moving toward her. He wouldn't force her if she wasn't interested but would pull back.

"I'm going to kiss you, Sierra," he said softly. "Say no and I'll stop." He hoped and prayed she didn't.

"Stop talking and just kiss me," she said softly, pulling him closer.

His heart felt as though there was a steam train chugging along in his chest, and fireworks went off in his head. He was in heaven.

As their lips met, a thrill went down his spine.

His hands went up to her cheeks, and he cupped her face. She returned the kiss with as much fervor as he'd hoped. Perhaps more.

He rested his head on her shoulder for long moments contemplating their future together, then nibbled at her neck in the silence of the night. He'd always loved it up here, and Sierra was the only one he'd ever brought here. They'd made so many memories together, and he wasn't prepared to tarnish them.

Now he wanted to make new memories with her.

He pulled her closer and enveloped her in a hug. Not a hug of friendship, but a hug that affirmed his love.

"I've never stopped loving you," he whispered.

She pulled back suddenly.

"It was a bad idea to come up here," she said quickly. "Nothing is decided, and I don't want to start something we might not get to finish.

He stared into her eyes in the moonlight. "I'm not starting anything," he said quietly. "Rather picking up where we left off. It feels like we've never been apart."

"I know," she replied quietly, then rested her head on his shoulder again. "It's all too hard right now. All these difficult decisions are clogging up my brain and hurting my heart."

He put his arm around her again. "I don't want to make things harder. When you're ready, I'll be here for you."

For the next half an hour they stayed that way, holding each other close, all the time Braxton was hoping they had the rest of their lives together.

Chapter Eight

He left the coffee shop the next morning and headed to where he knew Sierra would be.

The same place she'd been every day for the last week – at Evelyn's place.

"Nice going, Braxton," Mrs Sheridan called from outside her florist shop. She gave him a thumbs up.

He frowned. What was she on about? He had two coffees in his hands – one for himself, and the other for Sierra. That surely couldn't be what she meant.

He crossed the road. "Looking forward to it, Brax." This time it was Shelley from the news agency.

He mentally scratched his head. "Hey, Shelley," he said, then continued walking.

"Hooley Dooley, I can't wait," said Mrs Halligan, the butcher's wife.

Braxton was totally confused. *What on earth was everyone on about?*

He finally arrived at his destination. He knocked then stood back. Sierra greeted him with a genuinely welcoming smile. "Just what I need! You are such a life-saver," she said.

Putting the confusion of the last few minutes behind him, Braxton sat down beside her as she sipped her coffee.

"How is it going?" She looked frazzled, confused. Almost beat.

"I think I'm going to have to get an accountant in. Some of these figures are rather confusing. Besides," she leaned back on the chair. "I'd rather be doing something productive than fiddling about with figures for days on end." She sighed.

"Oh, I heard back from the real estate agent. He's already got a buyer for my unit. *If* I decide to sell that is. Good price too."

He frowned. He hated to think of her selling her home if this didn't work out. "I can lend you the money," he said quietly but firmly. "Please think about it," he said quickly when she frowned. "I honestly don't mind. Another thought – I could become a silent partner?"

She glared at him. *Had he offended her?*

"For your information," she said, stabbing a finger at his chest. "I don't need your money. I don't *need* to sell my unit, but I'd rather do that and have plenty of capital behind me for the start up."

She looked annoyed. Really annoyed. It was all he could do to stop himself from grinning.

She was cute when she was mad. He'd forgotten that.

Braxton put both hands in the air as a defense mechanism. "Whoa. I didn't mean to offend you."

She looked down to the ground. "Sorry. I guess I got a bit carried away." She took another sip of her coffee and went back to her books.

He watched as she scribbled away in her notebook, then leaned back looking defeated.

"If it helps, I could call my accountant for you?"

She spun around. "Oh, would you? That would be wonderful!" She leaned across and hugged him. He wasn't going to refuse her affections.

"This is so hard, Brax," she said into his ear as she rested her head on his shoulder.

He held her tight. "I'm sorry. This is my fault," he said quietly. "I suggested it."

She shook her head. "I'm really glad you did, but I thought I could do all the calculations myself. It's just too big a job, and I've got so much on my mind."

She leaned back away from him and he felt bereft. He knew he was getting too close for comfort, especially if she ended up leaving again. He was trying to keep his distance, but it wasn't working.

He had already fallen in love with her all over again.

* * *

"**I**'ve been doing some research."

Braxton had insisted on taking Sierra to the local historical society. She was confused at first, but suddenly it all became clear.

He handed her a pair of white gloves, putting on a pair himself, then opened an obviously antique book - it had to be at least one hundred years old. He pointed to a very tarnished article. "Oh my gosh, that looks like Gran's place!"

Adrenalin rushed through her veins. "But it surely can't be," she said. "That place is an inn." She squinted and looked closer.

Braxton sat there grinning.

She read the article. "It *is* Gran's place! It was an inn when it was first built in 1885. Oh my gosh." She felt as though all the air had been knocked out of her lungs.

"How is it not historically listed?" she whispered, for fear someone might hear.

Brax leaned in. "Oversight I'd say." He straightened his shoulders and sat back. "You could use this information as a drawcard. I thought you'd be interested."

"I am indeed."

She continued to read the article. "This changes everything," she said, a tingle running down her spine. "I'll contact the architect and make sure everything is era specific."

She turned the pages carefully. Her eyes scanned the photographs depicting the Oakdale Inn with its very prestigious guests arriving in their impressive carriages. "This is so exciting!"

She turned to Brax and hugged him tight. "You're amazing," she said. "No wonder I love you."

She suddenly slapped her hands to her mouth and stared at him. "I didn't mean..."

"It's fine, don't think about it for another minute," he said. But his words sounded injured. As though she'd just broken his heart.

But she knew what she'd said was true. She did love him and could never love another. She dearly didn't want to leave Oakdale, so she had to find a way to stay.

* * *

He was being selfish. Braxton knew he was.

But he also knew the moment he told Sierra about the old inn, she wouldn't back away. She loved that old house more than life itself.

She'd told him so more times than he could recall. And not only when they were teenagers – since she'd arrived back home.

Back home...

Oh, how he hoped that were true. She'd confided that she'd always considered Oakdale her home, despite living in the city for more than a decade.

Deep down she was a country girl. Had always been a country girl. He had no idea how she'd managed to stay away for so long.

With all the flurry of activity surrounding Evelyn's house, he'd been pushed to the backburner. His heart fluttered.

He'd been pushed aside for a house. He felt jealous of that house. It made him chuckle to think he was competing with a house for her affections.

When she was ready, Sierra would tell him her intentions, would tell him her final decision.

He was not going to try and influence her; she needed to make her own decision without him trying to force her hand. If she stayed, he wanted her to stay of her own volition.

And oh man, he truly wanted her to stay.

Sierra was his soul mate. Would always be his soul mate. If it meant uprooting his entire life and moving to the city to be with her, that's what he would do.

Austin could run the property without him. He was more than capable, he'd proven that time and again.

He was not prepared to lose her again.

* * *

Braxton's accountant had been a huge help.

He'd done all the number crunching, while she'd contacted the suppliers to get firm prices.

Everything was finally falling into place.

And now?

The old house, Gran's house, had become a Mecca of activity.

Everything changed the moment Sierra knew the house had once been of historical significance to Oakdale. The architect was notified, and he put everything into place.

This was going to happen. One way or another, she was going to ensure this beautiful old building received the respect it deserved.

Gran would be so pleased. She'd be up there in heaven dancing at the prospect.

Sierra's eyes welled. Her dear old Gran would have loved to see this place restored to its former glory. Would have reveled in being a part of it. It was a great shame they didn't know about this before – Sierra would have funded the restorations without a doubt.

The Historical Society of Oakdale would help ensure the renovations would be appropriate and put Sierra on the right track to get it historically listed. She wanted to do the right thing. Wanted to ensure its future.

With all this frenzied activity, she'd pushed Braxton to the back of her mind. At least that's what she thought she'd do. But Braxton had never been far from her mind. Ever.

The past ten years had been hell. Gran had wanted the best for her and sent her away 'to the big city' to make a life away from Oakdale. Away from Braxton.

Gran had adored Braxton, she'd often told Sierra what a great young man he was, and how he would make a wonderful husband one day.

She'd worried Sierra and Braxton were getting too involved too quick, and it would tie Sierra down, without her having a chance to experience her own life. And she'd loved her for it.

It had opened up a whole new world for Sierra – one she didn't know existed. She'd studied hard, worked hard, and made it in a traditionally man's world.

She had it all – a prestigious job and money. More money than she could ever use.

But in the process, she'd lost the love of her life.

And now? Now she was going to make it right. She was going to fix Gran's house until it was restored to its former glory.

Braxton was a whole different story. Somehow she had to make that right too.

Chapter Nine

Braxton stood rigid in the center of the stage and braced himself.

Every muscle in his body was taut, and the hair on the back of his neck stood up.

He looked across the sea of women who were staring at him in anticipation. They held tight to their numbers; numbers on a stick they would use to bid with.

He groaned.

How did it come to this? Why did he let his cousin Melanie manipulate him into doing this?

Melanie had *volunteered him* to help out for the charity event but had left out crucial information. She failed to explain exactly what he would be doing.

It had only become clear when the advertising material had been distributed a few days earlier. When the town's people had begun to make strange comments.

He shook his head in disgust.

"Braxton, Braxton, Braxton!" The women were chanting and clapping at the same time.

He stared down at his feet. This couldn't be happening.

"Take off your shirt, Braxton," one woman yelled. "Let us see your yummy muscles."

His head shot up and he felt the color drain from his face.

"Come on," another woman said. "I know you like it. You are so sexy!" A slow grin crossed his face at her words.

He'd never thought about himself as sexy, but hell, he'd take it any day.

Without taking his gaze from her, he slowly pulled off his jacket and flicked it to the floor. The resulting noise was deafening.

"More, more, more!" The chanting began again.

He swallowed hard. As much as he was annoyed with Mel, he was enjoying his ten minutes of fame.

"Take it off, take it off, take it off." A spotlight suddenly focused on him, standing up there on the stage.

He swallowed again, flexed his well sculptured muscles, then grabbed the bottom of his tight-fitting t-shirt and slowly pulled it up over his head, revealing his well-built body. He then tossed the shirt aside. His muscled chest and arms were bare for all to see.

The cheering and chanting became an uproar. He scanned the room until his gaze landed on his cousin's smug face.

She had that 'told you so' look about her.

"You'll fetch at least two thousand," she'd told him when he discovered what she'd done. He had his doubts.

His heart rate amplified as the bidding began.

Not in his wildest dreams did he ever imagine he would be part of a bachelor auction.

As the bidding began, Braxton's gaze scanned the room.

He could see women, young and old, waving their numbers about. The bidding had started at five hundred and was now at the fifteen hundred mark. He tried to put it out of his head.

It was like a meat auction, only the highest bidder got to have him for a date night. There was only one person he wanted to take on a date, and that was Sierra.

But for the youth of Oakdale, he would endure that one date. Hopefully it was one of the older ladies in town. They'd be easy to please and wouldn't hit on him.

He grinned.

"Braxton, take it all off!"

Good grief. Did old Mrs Perry really just say that? "Not likely," he yelled back.

The Master of Ceremonies stood at the side of the stage with a microphone. "Now then ladies, calm down," he said. "We know Braxton Chalmers is the catch of the century, but we need some decorum. Please."

He looked across at the man of the moment and grinned. Braxton almost died with embarrassment.

"Two thousand," the MC said. "Anyone willing to go above two thousand?" He glanced around the room.

Another number went up. "Thank you, Mrs Peterson. Do I have any more bids? Just look at this prize." He pointed across at Braxton. "Voted Bachelor of the Year several times, you won't want to let this bachelor get away."

Braxton wanted to melt into the floor boards. He glared across at his cousin, Mel. No doubt she put the MC up to this. Dragging up past history he wanted to forget.

He glared at her again, and she had the gall to grin and nod her head.

Where was Sierra? He scanned the room again, but she was nowhere to be seen. He was sure she'd be here to watch him at the height of his embarrassment.

He was furious when he'd discovered she'd known all along about Mel's scheme, but he couldn't stay mad very long. Especially once he found out Mel had sworn her to secrecy.

Thinking back on it, he couldn't blame her. Mel had been her best friend when they were growing up, and things hadn't changed. They were still as close as two peas in a pod. Almost inseparable. Like the two of them once were.

Besides, she probably thought it was a great joke.

He glanced to the side of the stage. There she was, standing, watching, and grinning broadly.

She wasn't bidding. At least he could be thankful for that. He wanted to take Sierra out on his terms. And to have her go willingly, not be forced because of some stupid bachelor auction.

"Five thousand dollars! Going, going, gone!"

Five thousand? Really?

He was really pleased. For the youth center of course, not his inflated male ego.

But who had the winning bid? Women were scurrying all over the place, making it difficult to see who had won. Who had bought him for a night? Who he was going to have to entertain?

The thought made him shudder.

He hadn't been paying attention. Hadn't taken enough notice of the proceedings. He could be stuck with anyone.

"Congratulations to Mrs Emily Petersen! Please go to the official at the back of the room and make arrangements for payment. The youth of Oakdale thank you. And you too, Braxton Chalmers." He felt the heat creep up his face. "You've been a good sport. Give him a hand everyone."

The room erupted into applause and wolf-whistling, and he slinked off the stage, grabbing his shirt and jacket, and giving a small wave as he left.

Thank goodness that was over. Braxton had never been so embarrassed in his life. At least he had some sort of redemption – five thousand was way more than he'd expected to raise. It was more than any of the other bachelor's had managed. At least he hadn't been embarrassed by some piddly little amount.

The moment he was off the stage, Sierra came to him. "You looked like you were enjoying yourself out there," she said.

"Never," he said, grinning like the Cheshire cat out of Alice in Wonderland. Only he had enjoyed himself. Mel told him he would, and he'd wanted to prove her wrong.

Only she was right.

She leaned forward and whispered in his ear. "You looked pretty sexy standing out there, half undressed, flexing your muscles for all those old ladies."

She straightened up, then stared into his eyes. "Get dressed. You don't have to impress me with your sculptured body." She laughed and began to walk away.

"I know they're putting supper on later," he said. "But I'm famished. And ready to leave. Want to join me?"

Chapter Ten

Braxton *really* did not want to do this.

He stood outside of *Angel's Kitchen* and stared through the window. He'd agreed to meet Mrs Petersen for dinner tonight as her reward for handing over five thousand dollars to the Youth Center.

Cudos to her. He helped in other ways, but to part with your hard-earned cash, that was pretty bold.

She'd called to say the dinner was arranged if the date suited him. He decided just to get it over and done with.

When he entered the restaurant, Joyce greeted him at the door. "It's so nice to see you again, Braxton," she said smiling. She even reached up and hugged him. "You're becoming a familiar face in here. I like that," she said.

She led him to a private room at the back of the restaurant. He was taken aback as he hadn't realized it even existed. They stopped when they arrived. The closed door had "private" printed on it.

She slowly opened the door, where Braxton expected to find Emily Petersen. Instead Sierra sat alone at the candlelit table.

"Sierra? What are you doing here? I expected Mrs Petersen."

She laughed. "I couldn't bid and support you on the stage at the same time, now could I?" She laughed again, and the headache that was threatening to form disappeared.

"It was you? I didn't think you'd be able to afford… I mean with all the other expenses…" He stopped. He wasn't getting his viewpoint across very well.

Joyce grinned, then turned to leave the room. She turned the lights down low before she left, then shut the door firmly.

"Mrs Petersen was happy to indulge me. It was a big adventure for her, she said."

He shook his head in disbelief.

"Sit. You're making me nervous."

He scraped the chair along the floor before sitting opposite her. "You're very crafty. I hadn't expected this."

"Oh. You're disappointed," she said lightheartedly.

He reached across the petal-strewn table and held her hand. Joyce had gone all out for them. "Not a bit. Totally the opposite in fact."

Joyce soon returned with a bottle of champagne and two glasses. She began to uncork the bottle, but Braxton interrupted her. "I can do that," he said. "Thanks."

The smug look on her face told him she'd read him like a book. He wanted to be alone with Sierra.

"There's a lot of activity going on at the inn," he said, no longer calling it a house.

She stared at him for a few moments, then brushed her loose hair behind her ear. "There is," she said. "Loads. Brax, I need to tell you something…"

He put his finger to her mouth. "I want to say something first." He didn't continue but waited for her acceptance. She nodded slightly, so he continued.

"I think by now you know what you mean to me, Sierra." He squeezed her hand gently and looked down at their entwined fingers. "We've known each other for such a long time. We basically grew up together."

She nodded again.

"I have no idea if you've made your decision yet, about whether you're staying or not."

She began to open her mouth, but he put his finger there again. "I need to say this now, or I might not say it at all."

"Fair enough."

"I love you, Sierra. I've spent the last ten years pining for you. I haven't been able to form relationships with other women because I missed you so much."

Her eyes opened wide in amazement.

He shuffled about in his seat. "I can't bear to think of you leaving again. Of you leaving me again." His voice was beginning to break. This was breaking his heart.

"Brax, I…"

"Please. I have to say this now, or I might never say it."

"Okay. Sorry."

He stared into her eyes. Her beautiful chocolate colored eyes that he couldn't bear to never see again. "I'm coming with you when you leave."

Her eyes opened wide. "But,"

"I love you, Sierra," he said, pulling his hand away and pouring the champagne. "I am willing to give up everything to be with you."

He reached into his pocket and pulled out a ring box. "Will you marry me," he said, opening the box to reveal an expensive diamond ring. "I'll follow you to the ends of the earth, even to the city," he said grinning. "I will not spend another ten years without you."

"Oh Brax," she said, running around to his side of the table. She hugged him tightly, then kissed him.

It was then the door to their private room opened. "Oops. Sorry. Am I interrupting something?" Joyce had a glint in her eye as if she absolutely knew she was.

Sierra quickly straightened.

"Braxton has asked me to marry him," she told the older woman with absolutely no emotion. His heart thudded in disappointment.

"Congratulations," she said excitedly. "I knew you two were meant for each other."

"She hasn't said yes," Braxton said dryly.

Joyce put down the tray of herb bread she was carrying. "What is wrong with you girl?"

"I didn't get a chance yet. You interrupted," Sierra said, laughing.

"So get to it! Are you going to marry this hunky man? If not, I'll happily take him." She left the room laughing.

Sierra sat down again, putting her hands in her lap. "It's a beautiful ring, Brax," she said, looking at the petals on the table.

He watched the flames dance across her face. She was going to refuse him. The writing was on the wall. His heart shattered – he was going to lose her again. Was he such a terrible person?

"You have no idea how grateful I am for you finding out about the original inn. The work is coming along nicely, and we should be open in about four months."

His heart was beating so rapidly, he felt light-headed. He was convinced she was about to refuse him.

"I don't have as much leave as I need to see the project through."

The thumping in his head was making it hard to concentrate. He felt sick. He'd put his heart on the line and it was about to be ripped apart.

"So it's no then." He began to stand. He couldn't do this.

"Brax," she whispered. "Hear me out."

It was the least he could do. They'd been friends for far too long for him to walk out on her now.

"I want to see this project through. Honestly, I couldn't have done it without you. Any of it. I know Gran would be so happy with what we've doing."

"But you're not staying. Like I said, I'll follow you to the ends of the earth. If you want me that is." His emotions were taking over, and his voice was a mere whisper.

"Brax," she said softly. "I love you. I'm not going anywhere – I've resigned."

His head shot up. "You resigned? You really resigned?" His breathing was shallow, and he couldn't think straight.

Then he realized she hadn't agreed to marry him. "I'm confused. Is that a yes?"

"It's a yes!" The candlelight danced across her face and his heart was dancing too. He couldn't believe he was finally going to be with the one he loved. The only one he'd ever loved.

Joyce tapped lightly on the door. Braxton jumped up and opened it for her. "She said yes!" he said excitedly, then leaned down and kissed the surprised woman on the cheek.

"Of course she did," Joyce said. "It was obvious you two love-birds are deeply in love. Now, open your menus."

Chapter Eleven

Four Months Later

Mel put the finishing touches to Sierra's make up, then placed the veil on her head.

"This is sooo exciting! I can't believe you two are finally getting married."

Sierra grinned at her. Even after all the preparations, it was still hard to get her head around.

There was a knock at the door. "That better not be Braxton," Mel quipped. "He's not allowed to see you before the wedding."

She opened the door a touch and put her head around it. "Oh hello," she said. "Hang on a tic. I think she's ready." She closed the door again and turned to Sierra. "It's the photographer. Are you ready to take the plunge?" She grinned.

She'd been grinning since the moment they'd told Mel they were getting married.

Sierra had made a condition – she wanted the wedding at the newly restored inn.

It was for Gran. She would have been beside herself with joy if she'd been here today. But Sierra knew in her heart that Gran was there with her, looking over her.

"Don't you dare!" Mel screeched. "Don't you dare cry! You'll mess up your make up."

She couldn't help it. She dearly wished Gran was here today, to give her away. Instead, the only other person she considered family was doing that job. And she was standing in front of her right now.

"Oh my, you've made me cry too," Mel said. She reached for the make up removal wipes, then went to the door. "Just give us a minute. We've had a make up disaster," she explained.

What he thought of that, Sierra dare not think.

A few minutes later and their *faux pas* was erased and repaired. Thank goodness for Mel. She might be bossy, but she had everything under control, including the foyer where the wedding was to take place.

The brand-new Oakdale Inn was not in operation yet but would be officially opened in a few days time.

Sierra's new chef was catering for the day, and he promised to be outstanding and a big drawcard to the inn. So what if she'd poached him from the hotel she used to manage? They had plenty of others. But this one was the crème de la crème.

They spent the next thirty minutes having bridal photographs taken. Sierra was so pleased she'd followed her heart and had both her dress and Mel's made to fit the era of the hotel. They really fit with the décor.

By the time the photography was finished, she could hear movement and voices downstairs. The guests must be starting to arrive.

And hopefully, her groom.

* * *

Braxton stood at the front of the foyer, which had been temporarily turned into a chapel, complete with a flower covered archway. He knew immediately that would have been Mel's doing.

She'd always been creative, and he could see her now – she would have been in her element.

Right now though, she'd be upstairs with his bride. He mentally kicked himself. He couldn't get used to the fact Sierra was about to become his wife.

A hush suddenly came over the place, and everyone looked toward the spiral staircase. As his Groomsman, Austin Addison looked upwards, he followed suit.

His beautiful bride was slowly descending the stairs, her long wedding trail flowing behind her. He'd thought her crazy when she said her dress was going to suit the era of the original inn. She'd had to have it specially made, but now, taking it all in, he could see why she did.

Mel was fussing with the train as they got closer to the archway, but she was grinning.

They'd invited Joyce Kingston, the owner of *Angel's Kitchen*. They'd frequented the restaurant since that night and become quite close to Joyce. She eventually revealed that she and Evelyn were close friends and had been for some years.

Braxton stared at his bride as she came toward him. Her beauty overwhelmed him. She was even more beautiful now than she was ten years ago. But it was her internal beauty that had originally taken him in. She was very special, inside and out.

As he reached for her hand, he glanced across at his parents. His mother was crying. Not that he'd expected anything less. He felt for Sierra at that moment – her parents were long gone, and sadly, so was the amazing woman who had brought her up.

He felt a tingle go down his spine. She was here, he knew she was, looking over them both and giving them her blessings.

Hands entwined, they turned toward the preacher.

It seemed like forever before they became husband and wife.

Epilogue

Twelve Months Later

"Cassie, can you pass me those booking sheets, please?"

Although she didn't have a lot to do with the thriving inn these days, Sierra still liked to keep her hand in. Cassie Somerton was her manager and kept everything running smoothly.

Philippe, her poached chef, was the best in the business, and people came from far and wide to try his food. As she'd predicted, he was a major drawcard, but even more was the fact they were able to stay in a genuine nineteenth century inn. One that had been beautifully restored to its former glory.

"Seriously? You're still going to do this," Cassie asked. "I'm more than capable of checking them over." She handed them across anyway.

Sierra pushed her hair back behind her ear. "You know it's not a question of your ability," she said quietly. "I just like to keep a hand in."

Cassie put her hands to her hips. "I'm not trying to be insolent," she said. "But look at yourself." She stared at Sierra's very swollen belly. "You're ready to drop your bundle."

"I have a few days yet," Sierra retorted. "I can do this."

Cassie stared at her, then snatched up her cell phone. "I don't think so," she said. "Your waters just broke."

Sierra looked to the floor – Cassie was right.

"Braxton," Cassie said. "It's time. Sierra's waters have broken. Get to the hospital pronto. Calm down," she told him. "For a grown man, you're acting like a scared teenager." She grinned at Sierra and ended the call.

"Right, hospital for you. Braxton is going to meet us there."

* * *

"It's about time you arrived," Sierra said, trying to breath through another contraction. "I've been here for hours. Where have you been?" She looked really annoyed.

He glanced at Cassie, then back to Sierra. "Sweetheart," he said gently. "It's not even half an hour since Cassie called."

"It feels longer." She grabbed his hand. "Oh boy." She breathed rapidly, and the midwife came in to check her over.

Cassie left them alone.

"Are you the dad?" She glared at Braxton, as though this was all his fault. Okay, it *was* his fault, but Sierra had a part in it too.

He nodded. "Yep. Braxton Chalmers," he said proudly. He still couldn't believe he was going to be a father soon. Probably in about twelve hours?

"Right then Braxton. Brace yourself. We're going to the delivery room. Your baby is on the way." He felt as though he'd been punched.

"On the way. Like, now on the way? I thought..."

She smiled for the first time. "Don't think. Babies have a mind of their own, and this one is ready to meet its parents."

A wheelchair was brought in, and Sierra gently placed in it, a blanket draped over her legs. She looked up at him, her expression unreadable. A mix of both anticipation and fear. He reached for her hand again. "I'm not going anywhere," he said quietly, then leaned down and kissed her cheek.

Once settled, Sierra seemed to relax. At least as much as she could be between contractions. The midwife stayed with her the whole time.

Then suddenly the room was a buzz of activity. Braxton was given a gown to wear and was instructed not to faint. As if he would!

Plenty did, the midwife told him. He was determined that wouldn't happen to him. Besides, he'd delivered plenty of foals, why would this be any different?

Sierra let out a mighty scream, and the midwife checked her again. "The head is showing," she said. "It won't be long now."

Braxton looked across to see Sierra crying. "I can't wait to meet our baby," she said between tears. She reached up and wiped the tears from his face.

"Get ready to push!" The midwife gently gave instructions through the whole process and kept them informed. "Okay, push."

Sierra squeezed his hand tightly.

"Push again."

Sierra grimaced.

"One more. Come on, you can do it." She encouraged Sierra, even though she was exhausted. "Your baby is nearly here," she whispered.

Sierra pushed and screamed at the same time.

Braxton reached over and hugged Sierra when their baby began to cry. "It's a boy," the midwife announced.

A boy. They had a son. *Cody Jacob Chalmers.* The name they'd chosen together.

"Say hello to your baby boy." He'd been checked over, then wrapped tightly and was handed over to Sierra. "You keep a hand on him, dad. Sierra is very tired now."

She left them alone to get to know their new baby son.

All was right with the world now. He had the love of his life by his side, along with his beautiful new son.

Right then he knew Evelyn was looking over their shoulders, pouring her love over her great-grandson.

<u>The End</u>

BOOK 2 – Melanie's Story will be available soon on Amazon

Thank you so much for reading my book – I hope you enjoyed it.

I would greatly appreciate you leaving a review on Amazon, even if it is only a one-liner. It helps to have my books more visible on Amazon!

You might like to read about Braxton's cousin Melanie. Her story can be found here.

All my books can be seen on my [Amazon Author Page.](#)